Here Come Poppy and Max

by
Lindsey Gardiner

Little, Brown and Company
BOSTON   NEW YORK   LONDON

For my Mum and Dad – you're simply the best

Copyright © 2000 by Lindsey Gardiner

First published in Great Britain in 2000 by Orchard Books

First U.S. Edition

ISBN 0-316-60346-5

Library of Congress Catalog Card Number 99-44287

10 9 8 7 6 5 4 3 2 1

Printed in Singapore

This is
Poppy.

This is
Max.

Poppy wants to be like all
her favorite animals. She...

walks **tall**

like a giraffe,

splashes

like a duck,

waddles

like a penguin,

roars

like a tiger,

leaps

like a leopard,

stands

on one leg

like a flamingo,

bounces

like a kangaroo, but . . .

. . . her favorite animal of
all is Max, her dog.

And he loves Poppy
just the way she is.